Adapted by Kitty Richards

Based on the series created by Dan Povenmire & Jeff "Swampy" Marsh

Copyright © 2011 Disney Enterprises, Inc. All rights reserved. Published by Disney Press, an imprint of Disney Book Group.
No part of this book may be reproduced or transmitted in any form or by any means, electronic or mechanical, including
photocopying, recording, or by any information storage and retrieval system, without written permission from the publisher.
For information address Disney Press, 114 Fifth Avenue, New York, New York 10011-5690.
Printed in the United States of America
First Edition
1 3 5 7 9 10 8 6 4 2
ISBN 978-1-4231-3732-0
G658-7729-4-11196

DISNEY PRESS
NEW YORK

It was the Day Before Christmas,

and Phineas and Ferb's parents had gone out, leaving the boys' older sister, Candace, in charge. Candace was sure she was about to catch her little brothers doing something wrong. But when she flung open Phineas and Ferb's bedroom door, they were just sitting in their beds.

"Let me see that!" Candace demanded, grabbing the to-do list Ferb was holding. Number one was to write letters to Santa.

"Think of all the wonderful things Santa does for us. And he never asks for anything in return," Phineas said. That gave him an idea!

Meanwhile, Perry the Platypus, who was not only Phineas and Ferb's pet but also a secret agent, was at his spy organization's Christmas party. But Perry had to leave early to pay his archenemy, Dr. Doofenshmirtz, a visit. As you may or may not know,

EVIL NEVER TAKES A HOLIDAY.

cRASh!

Perry burst through the wall of Dr. Doofenshmirtz's headquarters. The evil doctor was waiting for him. He trapped Perry in a tree stand with a string of lights. Then he showed Agent P his latest invention—the NAUGHTY-iNATOR. He hoped it would ruin everyone's Christmas!

At home, Phineas and Ferb had finished building an amazing rest-and-relaxation lounge for Santa on top of their house. It was awesome!

"I think it's time someone did something cool for Santa, to show him we appreciate everything he does for us," Phineas told his friends Isabella, Buford, and Baljeet.

Phineas grabbed a bullhorn. "All right, everyone," he shouted as a group gathered in front of his house. "Grab yourself some decorations and let's . . ."

". . . GET OUR GRATEFUL ON!"

OPERATION BRIGHT LIGHTS BIG BELLY

Back at his lair, Dr. Doofenshmirtz heard someone knocking.
He opened the door to reveal carolers singing holiday songs.
But the doctor wasn't impressed.

Dr. Doofenshmirtz reached out and pushed a button on his Naughty-inator. He was sick of all the Christmas cheer!

At that moment, the sky over Danville grew ominous. "Hey, what's with the clouds?" Candace wondered. Just then, a mailman strode over to the group.

"I'm sorry, kids," he said. "It looks as if everyone in Danville got their letters to Santa sent back. They've all been stamped 'naughty.'"

Phineas stared at the letter in his hands. "Santa thinks everyone in Danville is *naughty*? But how can that be?" he said to himself. He was crushed.

Phineas had been good all year. There was no reason why he should be on the naughty list! Then he had another idea. He gathered everyone at the local radio station to broadcast to Santa that there had been a terrible mix-up.

After the broadcast, the group headed back to Phineas
and Ferb's house. When they arrived, two elves were waiting
to greet them!

Unfortunately, the elves didn't have good news. They told the gang that the whole city had been declared naughty!
"Do you think it could be a mistake?" Phineas asked hopefully.

One of the elves carefully inspected the Naughty-or-Nice Meter he was holding. He looked very concerned. "According to these readings, it's as if the city *itself* is misbehaving!" he reported.

At Dr. Doofenshmirtz's lair, Agent P was struggling to break free. Just then, the holiday **CD** that he received as a gift at the Christmas party fell to the ground. Dr. Doofenshmirtz decided to put it on. As the singer on the **CD** hit a high note, the -inator fizzled out!

Agent P saw his chance to escape and quickly untangled himself from his snare. He trapped Dr. Doofenshmirtz in the tree stand and wrapped *him* in lights.

THE EVIL DOCTOR WAS FOILED AGAIN!

Suddenly, the elves received a "nice" reading on the meter!
"Christmas is back on, right?" Phineas asked.

But the elves told him that now there wasn't enough time for Santa to visit Danville this year.

Phineas wasn't about to let Christmas pass them by. "We're going to save Christmas! Who's in?" he cheered.

The elves smiled. Maybe Christmas *could* be saved!

Phineas's mission: to deliver all of Danville's gifts to help Santa! The gang quickly built a rocket-powered sled.

With the push of a button, the team blasted off into the frosty night. But Phineas couldn't see where he was going. Since everyone in town thought Santa wasn't coming, they had never turned on their holiday lights!

"Christmas is coming! Turn the lights on!" Buford yelled as he parachuted out of the sleigh. A few moments later, Danville's lights glowed brightly!

Soon, all of the gifts had been delivered.

"Great work, guys," Phineas said as everyone hopped out of the sleigh.

A few minutes later, the gang spotted smoke billowing from the roof of Phineas and Ferb's house! But the smoke wasn't caused by a fire. It was coming from the sauna at the rest-and-relaxation spa that Phineas and Ferb had built!

Just then, Santa opened the door of the sauna room and stepped out!

"We thought you weren't coming to Danville!" Phineas exclaimed.

"And pass up this cool rest stop you made me? Unthinkable!" Santa told him. Then he grabbed a letter out of his pocket and began to read it aloud.

"'You are one of my biggest heroes. All I want for Christmas this year is a chance to be like you. Thank you, Phineas Flynn.'"

"Well, kids, it's time for me to head home," Santa told them.
As the sleigh soared into the sky, the friends smiled. It was going to be a wonderful Christmas after all!